Secrets of the Vine

FOR YOUNG HEARTS

SECRETS OF THE VINE™ FOR YOUNG HEARTS
Copyright © 2002 by Bruce Wilkinson

Text adaptation by Rob Suggs
Illustrations by Sergio Martinez

Published in Nashville, Tennessee, by Tommy Nelson®, a Division of Thomas Nelson, Inc.

Scripture quoted from the New King James Version (NKJV).
Copyright © 1979, 1980, 1982 by Thomas Nelson, Inc., Publishers

Library of Congress Cataloging-in-Publication Data

Wilkinson, Bruce.
    Secrets of the vine for young hearts/Bruce Wilkinson and Rob Suggs ; illustrated by
Sergio Martinez.
        p. cm.
    Summary: A rhyming version of the Gospel teaching that Christians should be as
branches that will bear fruit through Jesus Christ.
    ISBN 1-40030-055-X
    1. Jesus Christ—Juvenile poetry. 2. Children's poetry, American. 3. Christian poetry,
American. [1. Jesus Christ—Poetry. 2. Christian life—Poetry. 3. American poetry.] I.
Suggs, Rob. II. Martinez, Sergio, ill. III. Title.

PS3623.I55 S43 2002
811'6—dc21

                                                                    2002025081

Printed in the United States of America

02 03 04 05 06 WRZ 5 4 3 2 1

Cover and interior design by Koechel Peterson Design, Minneapolis, MN.

Secrets of the Vine™

FOR YOUNG HEARTS

BRUCE WILKINSON
and ROB SUGGS
Illustrated by SERGIO MARTINEZ

www.tommynelson.com

A Division of Thomas Nelson, Inc.
www.ThomasNelson.com

"I am the true vine, and My Father is the vinedresser.
Every branch in Me that does not bear fruit He takes away;
and every branch that bears fruit He prunes, that it may bear more fruit. . . .
He who abides in Me, and I in him, bears much fruit. . . .
By this My Father is glorified, that you bear much fruit."

JOHN 15:1–2, 5, 8

"*I*'m the true vine," Jesus said to His friends,
"And My Father's the gardener who loves and who tends.
The people who know Me are branches so fine—
They bear precious fruit as they grow from the vine."

"So you hold on to Me as I hold on to you;
We'll delight in the wonderful things you will do.
And you'll do things for Me—that's your fruit and My joy,
So I'll look for much fruit from each girl and each boy."

*E*very word Jesus said was a gift of great worth,
But He shared something special His last week on earth.
For He chose us on purpose—both your life and mine—
To use all the secrets we find in the vine.

For the secrets, once found, bring us joy and great pleasure.
It's just like discovering fabulous treasure.
So listen to Jesus; be eager to hear,
And He'll whisper these wonderful words in your ear.

Now the vine is a plant that is healthy and strong,
And it pleases the gardener all the day long;
For it's lovely and lively, from leaf to the root,
And its branches are bearing such beautiful fruit.

So the vine is like Jesus—His life and His love,
And the gardener, His Father, is smiling above.
The gardener waters, and nurtures, and feeds,
And He lovingly cares for each one of our needs.

You're just like a branch, for you're growing each day
To behave more like Jesus in every way.
You're connected to Him like a branch to a vine,
And He clings to you also and says, "You are Mine."

So Jesus cares deeply for each part of you,
And the places you go, and the things that you do.
As a branch will grow outward, you'll go many places,
Do many new things, and see many new faces.

But still you're connected to Jesus, your vine.
You will do things for Him, and His goodness will shine.
For in all that you do, His love will soon show,
And you'll honor your Lord with the fruit that you grow.

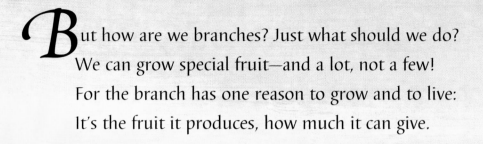

But how are we branches? Just what should we do?
We can grow special fruit—and a lot, not a few!
For the branch has one reason to grow and to live:
It's the fruit it produces, how much it can give.

And the fruit in your life is the way you behave
As you're helping and sharing, unselfish and brave.
And your fruit is your kindness when others are cruel.
It's obeying your parents, behaving at school.

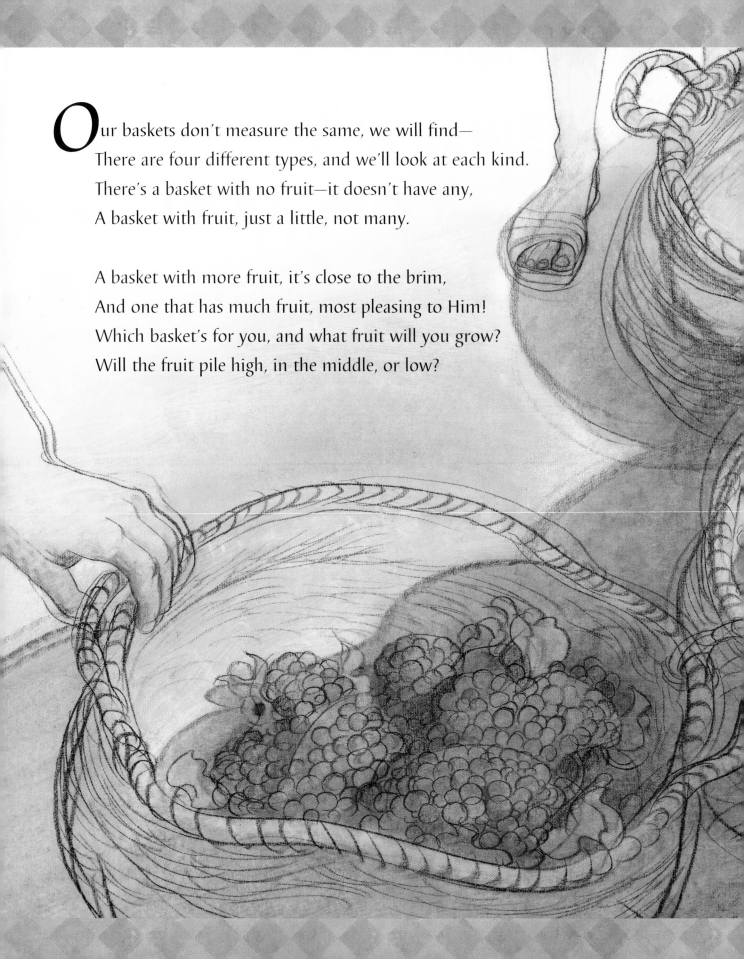

Our baskets don't measure the same, we will find—
There are four different types, and we'll look at each kind.
There's a basket with no fruit—it doesn't have any,
A basket with fruit, just a little, not many.

A basket with more fruit, it's close to the brim,
And one that has much fruit, most pleasing to Him!
Which basket's for you, and what fruit will you grow?
Will the fruit pile high, in the middle, or low?

*T*here are also three secrets to know and to share.

They depend on our choices, the fruit that we bear.

There are discipline, pruning, abiding—these three,

And they each make us wiser. Look closer and see . . .

There's a branch that grows weaker; it lies in the dirt,
And the gardener is sad, for it's trampled and hurt.
But He wants each branch to grow healthy and strong,
So He lifts it and cleans it and helps it along.

We are like fallen branches when we disobey,
When we do something wrong in our homes or at play.
But our best friend is Jesus, who knows how we feel,
And He'll gently correct us and help us to heal.

So whenever you've spoken some words that weren't nice,
Or you've done something wrong when you should have thought twice,
You can go make it right where you've done something wrong,
And let Jesus forgive you and help you along.

ut then, when the branch grows a little bit more,
The gardener plans an important new chore.
There is fruit—but how much? Not enough to please Him.
He will need to make room, so it's time for a trim.

For the branches grow quickly in every direction;
The gardener is wise as He makes His selection.
He trims needless stems with His delicate touch,
For He knows it increases the fruit very much.

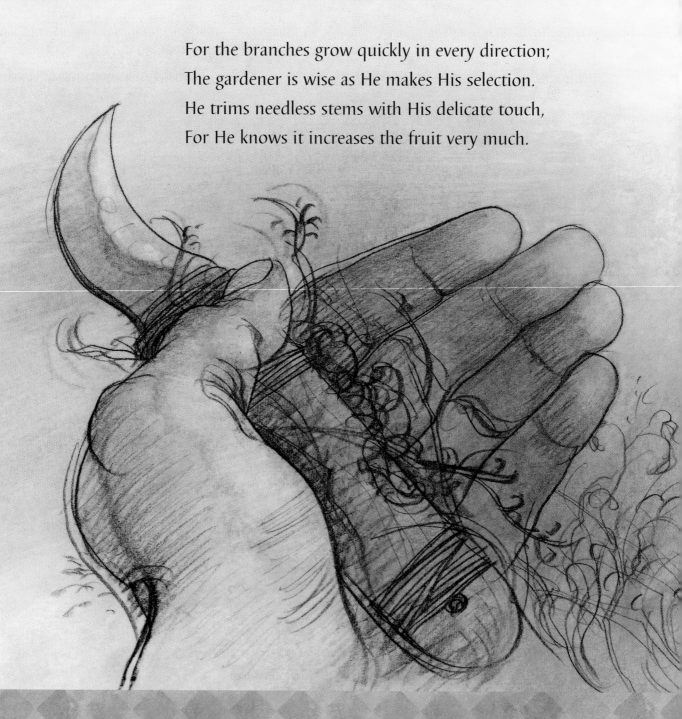

And in just the same way, Jesus helps us to choose.

There's the better to gain and the lesser to lose.

For your life will be busy, but here is the test:

Can you cut something out to make room for the best?

Can you find the activities dearest to Him?

He will show you the best, and He'll help you to trim.

You can ask this of Jesus: "Which way should I go?"

And He'll guide each decision and help you to know.

*B*ut there's one final secret—He saved it for last,
When the discipline times and the pruning are past.
There are branches whose fruit is abundant and fine—
They're the branches most close to the wonderful vine.

For the vine provides water and healthy nutrition,
Preparing you well for your fruit-bearing mission.
The branch and the vine stay together—*abide*.
That's a word that explains they're connected inside.

Abiding in Jesus means being His friend.
You'll be striving to please Him, beginning to end;
And your fruit will increase as your love for Him grows,
So your basket is full and it soon overflows.

You will love Jesus better each day that you live
And be eager to see how much fruit you can give.
You can bear special fruit that's so full and so fine;
It's the wonderful secret of Jesus, the vine.

"I am the true vine, and My Father is the vinedresser.
Every branch in Me that does not bear fruit He takes away;
and every branch that bears fruit He prunes, that it may bear more fruit. . . .
He who abides in Me, and I in him, bears much fruit. . . .
By this My Father is glorified, that you bear much fruit."

JOHN 15:1–2, 5, 8